Keesha

Momma's cooking dinner,
making my favorite foods:
jambalaya with corn bread.
And I get to help.
I sprinkle spices in the pot
and they dance and twirl
in Momma's thick sauce
as she stirs all the ingredients
with her wooden spoon.
Momma says soon it'll be time to eat.
And I can't wait 'cause I know
it's going to taste so good.

Tommy

I do not like sharin' a room with my older brother.
His clothes take up all the space in the closet.
He gets three of the dresser drawers
and I only get one.
His posters cover most of the wall.
And he gets the bottom bunk.
But worst of all, he snores.
Tonight I was dreamin' about havin' my own room.
But now I'm wide awake.

Keesha

I have sixteen teddy bears.
My momma's been collecting them
since the day I was born.
My black bear is the biggest of them all.
His marble eyes watch over me at night.
My pink teddy bear listens to all of my secrets.
And I always choose one to sleep with.
My older brother and sister say I'm too old
to sleep with
teddy bears.
But my momma
says it's okay and she
buys me another one.
Now I have seventeen.

Michael

I love sitting under the tree in front of my house.
Sometimes I sit under this tree all by myself
and I draw pictures.
Today, I sit under my tree
and I draw my neighbors.
Adrienne asks me if I want to play at her house.
I'll go over later.
Right now I am drawing pictures
and sitting under my favorite tree.
It's giving me all the shade I need to keep cool.

Adrienne

The calm before the storm
is what my granny calls it.
The sky don't look gray at all.
Seems like the sun is gonna shine forever.
Granny says that even though it don't look like it,
a storm's on the way.
So Keesha has to go home.
But soon, the storm will be over
and we'll be outside playing again.
The sky don't look gray at all.
Seems like the sun is gonna shine forever.

Tommy

My daddy's boardin' up the house
'cause the man on the news said a storm is comin'.
Don't know why he wants to save this house.
It's raggedy.
Sometimes when it rains,
the water comes through the roof.
Hits me on my head. Makes puddles on the floor.
I watch my momma pack.
We're leavin' tonight. Goin' to my aunt's house.
Momma tells me I can bring
two of my favorite things.
I can't wait to leave New Orleans.
Road trip with my family.
Houston is just five hours away.

Adrienne

Granny says they named the storm Katrina.
Hurricane Katrina.
She's coming to New Orleans
with her big wind and heavy rain.
Even though my granny said we weren't leaving,
we packed up our stuff today.
We're going to Baton Rouge.
Gonna stay with my granny's friend.

Michael

Tommy's family packed up and left.
And Adrienne is leaving too.
I give her the picture I drew yesterday.
Guess we're not playing together tomorrow.

Tommy

We've been sittin' in traffic for one whole hour.
Just sittin' and listenin' to the news on the radio.
I wanna hear my favorite song,
but my father says we need to know what's goin' on.
I wish the cars would move so we can leave.
I am tired of sittin' in this crowded car.
Houston is just five hours away,
but I don't think we're gettin' there no time soon.

Michael

Cars are turned upside down
and the street sign is floating in the water.
Daddy tells us to get to the attic
as fast as we can.
I take Jasmine's hand and I hold it tight,
like big brothers do.
She's too scared to look out the window,
but I'm not.

I look out the window
and I see the whole block swimming in water.
Furniture, clothes and toys are swirling in the flood.
Roofs are crumbling and windows are shattering.
Big winds have come and trees are breaking.
And all I can see is more water rising.
So I look away and I squeeze Jasmine's hand
real tight because now I am scared too.